The Circus Baby

The Circus Baby

A PICTURE BOOK BY
MAUD AND MISKA PETERSHAM

ALADDIN BOOKS

MACMILLAN PUBLISHING COMPANY • NEW YORK
COLLIER MACMILLAN PUBLISHERS • LONDON

Aladdin Books
Macmillan Publishing Company
866 Third Avenue, New York, NY 10022
Collier Macmillan Canada, Inc.
First Aladdin Books edition 1989
Printed in the United States of America
A hardcover edition of *The Circus Baby* is available from
Macmillan Publishing Company.

10 9 8 7 6 5 4 3 2

Library of Congress Cataloging-in-Publication Data
Petersham, Maud Fuller, 1890-1971.
The circus baby: a picture book/by Maud and Miska Petersham.   p.   cm.
Summary: The antics of Baby Elephant as his mother tries to teach him to eat with a spoon
at the clown family's dining table. ISBN 0-689-71295-2 (pbk.)
[1. Elephants—Fiction.] I. Petersham, Miska, 1888-1960. II. Title.
PZ7.P442Ci 1989   [E]—dc19   88-7369   CIP   AC

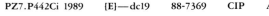

Once there was a Mother Elephant who lived with a circus.
Her baby marched beside her in every parade.
Sometimes when the sun was very very hot,
the tired little elephant would stop short.

He would not take another step.

For Mother Elephant this was most embarrassing.
She had to pick him up with her long trunk
and carry him. But all in all
Mother Elephant was very proud of her baby.

Mother Elephant was friendly
with all the people in the circus.

Best of all
she loved Zombie the clown and his family.

She spent much of the time with her
head poked through the flap of Zombie's tent.
Her tiny black eyes saw everything.

Her ears were so big
she could hear everything.

She liked to watch the clowns when they were eating.
Mr. Clown sat at one end of the table with
Mrs. Clown at the other end.
The baby clown, with a pretty bib tied around his neck,
sat in a high-chair in the middle.

Mother Elephant decided that her baby must learn
to eat properly just as the circus people did.

One day when Mr. and Mrs. Clown
were still in the big circus tent,
Mother Elephant awakened her child.
"Shush," she said to the sleepy baby.
"Come with me,
but don't make any noise."

The little elephant took hold of his mother's tail.
Stepping softly, they made their way
across the circus grounds.
They tiptoed right up to the clowns' empty tent.

After Mother Elephant and her baby
were both inside the tent,
she was surprised at how little space there was.
But she was very careful not to break anything.
She held her big flappy ears close to her head
and she made herself just as small as possible.

She sat her baby up on Mr. Clown's stool.
The baby clown's high-chair was much too small.

She tied Mrs. Clown's apron
around his neck for a bib.
In front of him she placed a bowl of beans
and the largest spoon she could find.

Now the little elephant always tried to do
what his mother wanted.
But he just could not manage that spoon.
He tried with one foot and then with another.
His trunk was always in the way.

At last he held the spoon with his trunk.
The beans spilled all over the apron-bib and
all over Mrs. Clown's nice clean tablecloth.

Mother Elephant coaxed him to try once more.

He put his foot out to hold the bowl.
The bowl tipped and clattered off the table.
Then Mr. Clown's stool gave a loud creak
and split into many pieces.

The Baby Elephant went tumbling to the floor.

Just at that moment
they heard Mr. and Mrs. Clown coming home.

Poor Mother Elephant!
She was so excited, she reared straight up.
The tent collapsed right over her head
and
right over the little elephant.

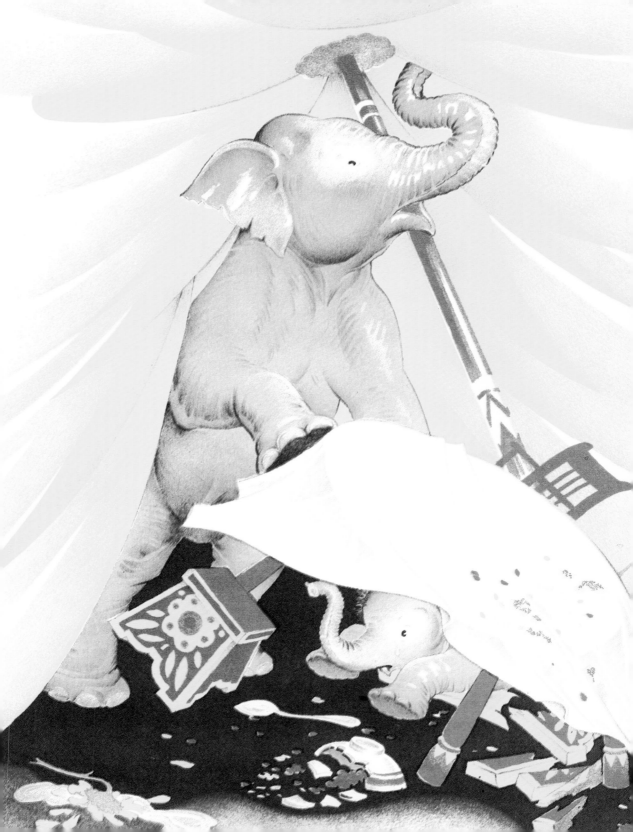

Then the surprised Mr. and Mrs. Clown
saw their tent
walk
away.

The next day Mr. and Mrs. Clown were given
a beautiful new tent. Mother Elephant
promised never to go into it.

And she said to her baby, "My child,
you do not have to learn to eat
as the circus people do because,

"after all, you are an ELEPHANT."